MH 4

Sassafras

Written by Stephen Cosgrove
Illustrated by Robin James

A Serendipity™ *Book*

PSS!
PRICE STERN SLOAN

The Serendipity™ Series was created by Stephen Cosgrove and Robin James.

Copyright © 1995, 1988 by Price Stern Sloan. All rights reserved.
Published by Price Stern Sloan, a division of
Penguin Young Readers Group, 345 Hudson Street, New York, New York 10014.

Library of Congress Catalog Card Number: 88-23645

ISBN 978-0-8431-3830-6

First Revised Edition
5 7 9 10 8 6

Dedicated to all the friends I left behind in Seattle. May the mountains echo with their laughter.

—*Stephen*

In the land of Serendipity there was a place of tangled vines and twisted trunks called the Jasmine Jungle. Birds flittered from tree to tree to look at all there was to see. Snakes and lions and zebras too, all lived in the wild and not in the zoo.

At the very edge of the Jasmine Jungle was a meadow of tall, swaying grass called the land of Savannah, where the zebras neighed in glee at the monkeys that swung in the trees.

The largest of the animals that lived in the land of Savannah were the elephants, the grandest of beasts. The elephants had large wobbily trunks that tasted the breeze and sometimes sneezed. They had large floppy ears that waved back and forth like fans to cool them on warm summer days.

One of these elephants was young, not more than a child, and was called Sassafras Tee. She had short, little legs that pounded the ground like drums beating rhythms into the air as she romped about the land of Savannah.

Sassafras was as normal as could be but she had one little, itty bitty problem—she always had to have the final word. Like an echo gone bad, she would repeat what everyone said.

If her mother said, "You'd better go to the river and wash up." Sassafras would sarcastically repeat in sing-song fashion, "Better go to the river and wash up!"

She would assume that no one heard her sarcastic remarks, but sarcastic remarks carry far and big-eared elephants have excellent hearing. That is why the other elephants didn't just call her Sassafras Tee, they called her Sassy because so sassy was she.

One morning, as the sun sleepily slipped over the trees of the Jasmine Jungle and the land of Savannah, Sassy was fast asleep, nestled in a pile of straw.

"Sassafras," her mother called, "get up, get up. It's time to get up. You don't want to be late for school!"

Sassafras tossed and turned and grumpily grumbled in her sing-songy voice, "Don't want to be late for school."

"What was that, dear?" her mother asked.

This echoing was a great little game for Sassy as she repeated her mother again, "What was that, dear?"

"You had better stop that now, young lady," her mother threatened.

As Sassafras skipped off to school she looked back and giggled, "Better stop that now, young lady." She sounded just like a naughty parrot.

Later that day, right after lunch, as she was sitting in the Jasmine Jungle School, Sassafras began a battle of wits that was the beginning of the end of the word war. As all the students were laughing and talking, the teacher, Mizz Mollie said, "Shhh! Everyone be quiet!"

Then Sassy echoed, "Everyone be quiet."

Mizz Mollie looked at Sassy and said again firmly, "Shhh! I mean everyone!"

Sassy looked about and quietly repeated, "I mean everyone!"

Mizz Mollie was becoming very angry indeed and as she glared at Sassy, her eyes kind of crossed the way teachers' eyes become when they get really mad, "Shhh! Everyone!"

Sassy looked around innocently and kind of crossed her eyes too and echoed, "Everyone!"

Mizz Mollie was very upset and wrote a note that she gave to Sassy as she sent her home from school. "Take this letter to your mother and don't come back to school until you stop this silly game."

Sassafras grabbed the note firmly in her trunk and as she skipped away down the path she could be heard to repeat over and over, "Take this letter to your mother . . . take this letter to your mother."

Her mother was upset that Sassy was sent home from school. She waved her trunk angrily and said, "This sassing has got to stop. There can be no more echoing of what others say."

Little Sassafras stood in the shadow of her mother, waved her trunk, and repeated innocently, "No more echoing of what others say!"

"That will be all, young lady!" her mother trumpeted as she flapped her ears angrily. "You will spend the rest of today bundling grasses all alone in the meadow. Now march!"

Sassy had never seen her mother so mad and she quickly did what she was told. She scooted down the path but couldn't resist an echoing snicker, "Now march, now march, now march!"

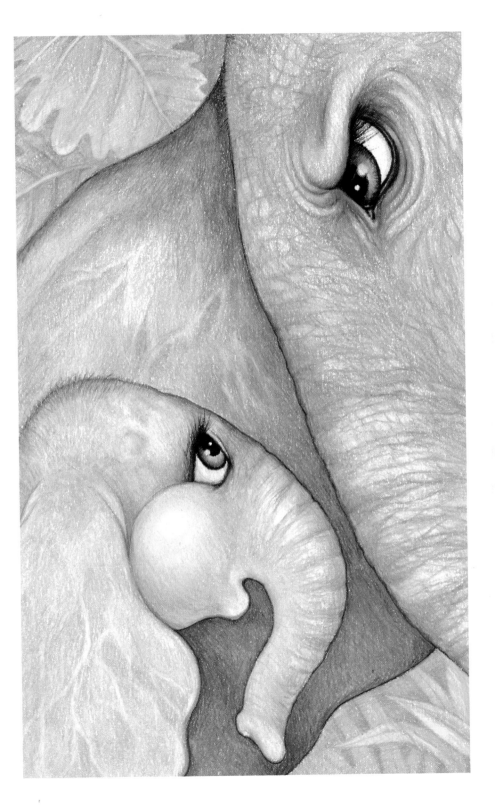

Sassy pretended to work in the meadow that day. Pretended to work, which was really play. She rolled some of the grasses into bundles and bales but then sat down and rested. She watched the birds that sailed in the warm winds that blew from the canyon just beyond the meadow.

The birds would scold and screech and Sassy would echo whatever noise they made. If the birds fluttered and flapped, Sassy would flap her ears and echo all that she heard. When the birds would scold and screech, Sassy would screech right back. No one would ever get the last word on Sassafras Tee.

As the sun was setting low, Sassafras went to the edge of the canyon and bellowed, "The world will never get the last word on me, for I am Sassafras Tee."

She turned to return to the herd but a gentle voice stopped her in her tracks. Off in the distance she could hear, "You can't get the last word on me . . . on me . . . for I am Sassafras Tee . . . Tee . . . Tee."

She wheeled around and looked and looked but there was no one there. "Humph," she said, "It was just the wind. For there is only one Sassafras Tee and that's me."

She had just turned to leave again when the voice called back, "It was just the wind . . . the wind. Only one Sassafras Tee and that's me . . . that's me . . . that's me!"

Sassy was becoming very angry. She stomped her foot and trumpeted loudly, "I am me! And you are just as ugly as can be for imitating me!"

She turned and tried to run away but the voice was quicker and bellowed on the wind. "You are just as ugly as can be . . . just as ugly as can be . . . imitating me . . . imitating me!"

The golden sun set lower and lower in the western skies, painting purple shadows on the canyon walls. Standing at the very edge of the canyon was a very frustrated little elephant with her curled trunk high in the air and a tiny tear tracing down her cheek.

Sassafras would have been standing there to this very day, had she not made a wondrous discovery. She discovered that if she said something nice, it would come echoing back a little bit better.

"Sassafras says, I'm sorry," she cried in a tiny voice.

Sure enough a tiny voice came back, "I'm sorry. I'm sorry . . . sorry . . . sorry."

She smiled and wiped her tear with her trunk and said again a little louder, "I'm so sorry and I promise to echo only good things from now on!"

Sure enough, as she turned away from the canyon walls, a voice echoed gently on the wind, "So, sorry . . . sorry. Promise . . . promise . . . good things . . . good things . . . good things. . . good things."

As Sassy walked back to the meadows of Savannah you could hear the echo go on and on and on and finally only the faintest hum of the gentle wind.

And if you looked very carefully on the edge of the canyon wall, you would have seen a tiny mouse whispering for all to hear:

SHE HAS ECHOED ... ECHOED ... echoed

SOMETHING NICE, YOU SEE ... YOU SEE ... you see.

NOW SHE'S NOT SASSY ANYMORE ... MORE ... more

BUT IS A LOVING SASSAFRAS TEE ... TEE ... TEE.

Serendipity™ Books

Created by
Stephen Cosgrove and Robin James

Enjoy all the delightful books in the Serendipity™ Series:

Available wherever books are sold.

PSS!
PRICE STERN SLOAN